To Tracy, my Muse and Inspiration.
And Doreen Lee, the first
and best editor I ever had.
Rest In Peace, Mum.
T. L.

For Kaya - grow strong,
little warrior.
S. H.

First published 2014 by Walker Books Ltd
87 Vauxhall Walk, London SE11 5HJ

2 4 6 8 10 9 7 5 3 1

Text © 2014 Tony Lee
Illustrations © 2014 Sam Hart

Coloured by Sam Hart with Flavio Costa

Lettered by Cadu Simões

The right of Tony Lee and Sam Hart to be identified as author and
illustrator of this work has been asserted by them in accordance with the
Copyright, Designs and Patents Act 1988.

This book has been typeset in CCWildWords

Printed in China

British Library Cataloguing in Publication Data:
a catalogue record for this book is available from the British Library

ISBN 978-1-4063-3615-3

www.walker.co.uk

MESSENGER

THE LEGEND OF JOAN OF ARC

MESSENGER

THE LEGEND OF JOAN OF ARC

WRITTEN BY
TONY LEE

ILLUSTRATED BY
SAM HART

COLOURED BY
SAM HART WITH **FLAVIO COSTA**

LETTERED BY
CADU SIMÕES

WALKER

The Hundred Years' War – where France and England fought for the ever-changing French throne.

One hundred and sixteen years of fighting, with small patches of peace. Generations lived and died knowing nothing else.

But then came the prophet, the messenger from God. The French began to fight back, scaring the English and forcing their allies to put her on trial for heresy...

...AND I WILL NOT REVEAL THOSE TO SAVE MY HEAD.

ORDER! ORDER, I TELL YOU!

AS YOU WISH. LET US MOVE ON. YOUR *CLOTHES*, CHILD.

DO YOU NOT FIND THAT A GIRL WEARING *MEN'S CLOTHING* TO TRIAL IS OF POOR TASTE?

THIS IS WHAT THE GUARDS *GAVE* ME. IF I HAD A DRESS, I WOULD WEAR IT.

OR WOULD THAT *HURT* YOUR CASE AGAINST ME? AFTER ALL, YOU CLAIM THAT A *WOMAN WEARING MEN'S CLOTHES* IS AGAINST GOD'S DECREE!

YOU'D RATHER WEAR MEN'S CLOTHING, *WOULDN'T YOU?* EASIER TO TRY TO *ESCAPE* AGAIN!

PLEASE, TRY - BECAUSE *ESCAPING FROM YOUR PENANCE* WOULD HAVE YOU *AUTOMATICALLY* CONVICTED OF HERESY *AS WELL!*

I DON'T RECOGNIZE YOUR *AUTHORITY,* BISHOP - YOU HELP THE *BURGUNDIANS,* OUR *ENEMIES,* WHO ARE ALLIED WITH *ENGLAND!*

AND I PLEDGED *NO OATH* THAT I WOULD NOT ESCAPE FROM MY ENEMIES, SO WHY SHOULDN'T I TRY? WANTING TO ESCAPE ISN'T *HERESY.* IT'S A PART OF BEING IN A *WAR.*

LET US TALK OF YOUR *CHILDHOOD.* BORN IN *DOMRÉMY,* YOU LIVED A NORMAL LIFE, DID YOU NOT?

YOUR FATHER, *JACQUES D'ARC,* WAS A VILLAGE OFFICIAL.

HE WAS A *FARMER,* YES – WE OWNED NEARLY FIFTY ACRES OF LAND.

HE WAS IN CHARGE OF THE LOCAL *MILITIA* AND COLLECTED THE TAXES, AMONG OTHER THINGS.

DOMRÉMY WAS – *IS* – LOYAL TO THE FRENCH, BUT AT THE TIME WAS SURROUNDED BY *BURGUNDIAN* TERRITORY.

WE WERE OFTEN RAIDED, ATTACKED BY BANDITS. ON ONE OCCASION THEY TRIED TO *BURN DOWN OUR VILLAGE.*

SO FROM AN EARLY AGE YOU WERE SURROUNDED BY SOLDIERS, WEAPONS?

FARMERS DEFENDING THEIR LAND AREN'T THE SAME AS *KNIGHTS IN ARMOUR,* BISHOP.

ALTHOUGH AS YOU *NEVER* VISIT THE VILLAGES, I'M NOT SURPRISED YOU *DON'T KNOW* THIS.

HA HA HA HA HA HA

TELL ME MORE ABOUT YOUR *UPBRINGING*. YOU'VE SAID THAT AS A CHILD, YOU WERE TAUGHT *PRAYERS*.

THE *PATERNOSTER*, *AVE MARIA* AND *CREDO* AMONG OTHERS.

YES, THAT IS TRUE.

COULD YOU REPEAT THE *PATERNOSTER* – THE *LORD'S PRAYER* – FOR US NOW?

OF COURSE, BISHOP – IT WOULD BE MY PLEASURE.

JUST AS SOON AS YOU HEAR MY *CONFESSION*, WHICH YOU HAVE *AVOIDED* THESE MANY MONTHS PAST.

YOU SEEM TO WANT TO MAKE ME OUT TO BE A WARRIOR FROM BIRTH – OR SOME KIND OF *HERETIC DEVIL CHILD* – BUT I LED A NORMAL LIFE.

AS A YOUNG GIRL I LEARNT TO SPIN AND SEW; I PLAYED AROUND THE *FAIRY TREE* WITH THE OTHER CHILDREN.

I CONFESSED MY SINS ONCE A YEAR...

...AND WHEN I WAS THIRTEEN, I HEARD THE *VOICE OF GOD*.

HERESY!

HERESY!

HERESY!

HERESY!

HERESY!

ORDER! ORDER, I TELL YOU!

JEHANNE! COME QUICK!

YOU'RE LATE FOR *DINNER!*

YOUR *FATHER'S* LOOKING FOR YOU.

I'LL BE RIGHT THERE, DURAND.

WHOOPS—

YOUR COUNTRY IS IN *PERIL*. FRANCE NEEDS A *MESSENGER FROM GOD*, A PROPHET TO HELP ITS PEOPLE IN THEIR TIME OF NEED.

YOU WILL BE THAT PROPHET.

I DON'T UNDERSTAND WHAT YOU MEAN – AM I TO *JOIN THE CHURCH*?

NO, YOU WILL BE *FAR MORE*. YOU WILL BE A BRIGHT *FLAME OF FAITH*, SHINING AGAINST THE DARKNESS.

YOU WILL *UNITE FRANCE* AGAINST AN ENEMY – AND REGAIN A *CROWN* FOR A KING.

BUT THE BRIGHTEST FLAMES *BURN OUT FASTEST*.

YOUR LIFE WILL BE A *SHORT* ONE. YOU WILL NEVER MARRY, HAVE CHILDREN – IT WILL BE A LIFE OF *HARDSHIP AND SCORN*.

BUT YOU WILL END IT BY *GOD'S SIDE*, EMBRACED BY *ANGELS*.

JEHANNE! ARE YOU ALL RIGHT? ARE YOU HURT?

I AM *FINE*, DURAND – JUST SCRATCHES AND BRUISES...

...BUT I FEAR I WILL *NEVER* BE THE SAME AGAIN.

YOUR COUSIN **WORRIES** US WITH NEWS OF YOUR ACCIDENT. ARE YOU SURE YOU'RE NOT HURT, JEHANNE?

I'M FINE, FATHER. THE **ANGEL** MADE ME BETTER, ANYWAY!

ANGEL?

WELL, MORE OF A **SAINT**, REALLY. MICHAEL. HE CAME WITH WORDS FROM **GOD**.

I'M GOING TO BE A **MESSENGER**. HE TOLD ME THINGS ABOUT MY FUTURE.

YOU DON'T FEEL **FEVERISH**, YET YOU'RE **DELIRIOUS**!

NOT AT ALL, MOTHER! GOD WILL **GUIDE** ME - EVERYTHING WILL BE OK!

I UNDERSTAND MY **ROLE** NOW.

ENOUGH!

JEHANNE, TO SPEAK THIS WAY ABOUT THE LORD IS **HERESY**. ONLY THE **POPE IN ROME** TALKS TO GOD! CHILD OR NO CHILD, YOU COULD BE **BURNT AT THE STAKE** FOR IT. IT'S NOTHING MORE THAN **WITCHCRAFT**!

I AM RESPONSIBLE FOR THE DEFENCE OF THIS VILLAGE AND I CANNOT HAVE A DAUGHTER THAT IS BELIEVED TO BE **DEVIL-TOUCHED**!

YOU MUST BE CONCUSSED. YOU WILL STAY IN BED UNTIL YOU ARE WELL AGAIN. UNTIL THESE "VOICES" ARE **GONE**.

A WEEK LATER.

JEHANNE! WHAT ARE YOU *DOING*? YOUR FATHER WILL KILL YOU IF HE CATCHES YOU *DISOBEYING* HIM!

I DON'T CARE WHAT FATHER SAYS! MICHAEL CAME TO ME, DURAND! THERE'S A *LAMB TRAPPED* AND SAVING HIM WILL LEAD TO BIGGER THINGS!

I'M SORRY, DURAND, BUT I *HAVE* TO DO THIS!

COME ON, WHERE ARE YOU?

BAAA!!!

THERE YOU ARE. STAY STILL; I'LL FREE YOU IN A MOMENT.

HOW DID YOU KNOW THE LAMB WAS *HERE*, JEHANNE? COULD YOU HEAR IT?

NO... IT WAS TOO FAR AWAY ... DURAND SAID YOUR *VOICES* TOLD YOU...

ACTUALLY, I **DON'T WANT** TO KNOW.

ALL THAT MATTERS IS THAT YOU **DISOBEYED** ME.

FATHER – I **HAD** TO! THE VOICES TOLD ME I HAD TO SAVE THIS LAMB TO GET YOU TO FOLLOW ME!

BECAUSE IF YOU **DIDN'T** FOLLOW ME...

"...I WOULDN'T BE ABLE TO **SHOW YOU THEM!**"

BURGUNDIAN RAIDERS! WE'D **NEVER** HAVE SEEN THEM IN TIME! WE HAVE TO WARN THE VILLAGERS!

JEHANNE, SAVING THIS LAMB MAY HAVE JUST **SAVED** DOMRÉMY!

RING THE CHURCH BELLS! INVADERS!

WE'RE BEING ATTACKED!

PULL BACK! *RETREAT!* THERE ARE NO PICKINGS HERE TODAY!

JUST THE CURSES OF A *GODLESS DEVIL CHILD!*

YEEAAHHH!!!! FLEE, YOU COWARDS!

TO MY *DAUGHTER!* WHO TURNED AWAY THE BURGUNDIANS WITH NOTHING BUT *WORDS!*

AYE, BUT SHE SHOULDN'T MAKE JOKES ABOUT *HEARING GOD.* THAT COULD GET HER *BURNT AS A WITCH.*

DON'T LISTEN TO HIM, CHILD. I DON'T KNOW HOW YOU DID IT, BUT IT WAS A *MIRACLE.*

AND THE CHURCH DOESN'T BURN PEOPLE WHO PERFORM MIRACLES.

BUT IT *WILL,* FATHER. IT WILL.

1427.

1428.

- SOB -

THANK YOU, LORD.

JEHANNE! JOAN! WHAT *EVER* IS THE *MATTER*, CHILD?

THE SAINTS, THEY'VE *SPOKEN* TO ME, FATHER HUGO.

THEY'VE TOLD ME WHAT I MUST *DO*. THEY'VE SHOWN ME MY PATH.

BUT SURELY THIS IS A *GOOD THING*, MY CHILD?

TO KNOW YOUR PATH, TO HAVE *GOD HIMSELF* GUIDING YOU?

YOU'D *THINK* SO, WOULDN'T YOU? BUT IF IT WERE, THEN THE CHURCH WOULDN'T CALL IT *HERESY*. THEY WOULDN'T *PUNISH* YOU.

GOD SPOKE TO ME. HE TOLD ME THAT I MUST BE HIS *MESSENGER*. THAT I MUST SPEAK FOR HIM.

FIGHT FOR HIM.

DIE FOR HIM.

BUT WHY? WHY WOULD GOD ASK SO MUCH OF *YOU*? YOU'RE JUST A *GIRL*!

I HAVE A MESSAGE FOR THE *DAUPHIN*, FATHER HUGO.

THE WAR AGAINST THE ENGLISH IS GOING *BADLY*. THE BURGUNDIANS ARE ALLIED WITH THEM AND THE FRENCH ARE *LOSING HOPE*.

I'M TO GUIDE HIS FORCES AGAINST THE *ENGLISH* AND HAVE HIM CROWNED *KING*. ALTHOUGH *HOW* I DO THAT, I HAVE NO IDEA.

THE ENGLISH HOLD *REIMS*, WHERE THE DAUPHIN NEEDS TO BE *CROWNED*. UNTIL IT IS WON BACK, FRANCE WILL *NEVER* HAVE A KING TO LEAD IT.

AND WITHOUT A KING, WE CANNOT HOPE TO *END* THIS WAR.

WELL, IF THIS IS WHAT YOU *BELIEVE*, THEN YOU MUST SPEAK TO THE *DAUPHIN* HIMSELF.

YES, FATHER.

I'LL JUST TRAVEL TO *CHINON* RIGHT NOW AND *ASK FOR AN AUDIENCE*!

YOU REASON WELL, CHILD.

HOWEVER, CHARLES'S FORCES ARE IN *VAUCOULEURS*, NOT FAR FROM HERE. PERHAPS THE GARRISON CAPTAIN, *ROBERT DE BAUDRICOURT*, COULD HELP?

OF COURSE! *HE'LL* KNOW THE DAUPHIN! HE COULD WRITE A LETTER OF *INTRODUCTION*.

WE WILL START THERE. *COMING*, FATHER?

NO, NO, *NO!*

I'LL NOT HAVE YOU TRAVEL INTO THE CENTRE OF A *WAR!* IT'S TOO DANGEROUS FOR A GIRL!

AND DOMRÉMY *ISN'T* ONE, FATHER? WE'RE *SURROUNDED* BY ENEMIES! UNTIL THE FRENCH FIGHT BACK, WE LIVE IN THE MIDDLE OF *ENEMY TERRITORY!*

EVERY WEEK BURGUNDIANS ATTACK US BECAUSE WE REMAIN LOYAL TO CHARLES!

TO STAY *HERE* IS JUST AS INSANE!

SHE HAS A POINT, JACQUES. WE CAN'T KEEP THIS UP FOR MUCH LONGER.

IT'S TRUE. THE ATTACKS HAVE *INCREASED* LATELY. BUT THIS IS NOTHING NEW!

SOON THEY WILL RELENT, AND WE'LL ENJOY A FEW MONTHS OF *PEACE* AGAIN!

AND WHAT IF THEY *DON'T*? WHAT IF THEY *SUCCEED* IN BURNING DOMRÉMY TO THE GROUND?

IT'S NOT JUST ABOUT THE *VILLAGE*. IF WE FALL, *ALL OF FRANCE* FALLS! WITHOUT ITS VILLAGES, FRANCE HAS *NOTHING!*

I CAN *STOP* THIS, FATHER. I CAN BRING AN END TO THE ATTACKS.

ALL I NEED TO DO IS SPEAK TO THE GARRISON CAPTAIN AT VAUCOULEURS; FATHER HUGO SAYS HIS NAME IS *ROBERT DE BAUDRICOURT.*

BAUDRICOURT WILL INTRODUCE ME TO THE DAUPHIN – AND CHARLES WILL LISTEN TO ME. HE *HAS* TO! AND THE WAR WILL CHANGE WHEN HE DOES.

FOR *FIVE YEARS* YOU'VE BELIEVED IN MY VOICES. PLEASE, BELIEVE IN THEM NOW.

THERE'S A HUGE DIFFERENCE BETWEEN HAVING A *LORD SAVE A VILLAGE* AND A *KING SAVE A COUNTRY.*

YOUR *FAITH* IN THE VOICES IS ADMIRABLE, BUT PEOPLE WON'T BELIEVE YOU. THEY'LL THINK YOU'RE MAD OR – WORSE – A *HERETIC.*

SO I WON'T LET YOU GO *ALONE.* DURAND, GO WITH YOUR COUSIN. ENSURE SHE RETURNS SAFELY. BY *FORCE* IF NEEDS BE.

YES, UNCLE.

THANK YOU, FATHER!

YES, YES ... NOW, GO ON WITH YOU. SAVE THE *VILLAGE,* SAVE *FRANCE,* DO WHATEVER YOU NEED TO DO. JUST COME HOME SAFE, YOU HEAR?

I'LL DO MY BEST, FATHER.

HAHAHAHA!

THANK YOU, CHILD. WE HAVEN'T HAD A GOOD LAUGH IN DAYS!

NOW, LISTEN HERE! MY COUSIN IS A *PROPHET FROM GOD!* SHE HAS SAVED OUR VILLAGE ON MORE THAN ONE OCCASION!

IF GOD SAYS SHE MUST SPEAK TO THE DAUPHIN — THEN *STEP ASIDE!*

YOUR COUSIN IS AN *IDIOT* WHO HEARS VOICES IN THE WIND. WE HAVE A DOZEN LIKE HER *EVERY WEEK*, TELLING US THE WORD OF THE LORD.

WE NEED *SOLDIERS*, NOT *MADWOMEN*. TAKE HER HOME...

...TAKE HER HOME TO HER FATHER AND GIVE HER A GOOD *WHIPPING*.

NOW LISTEN HERE—

THERE'S NO POINT, MY CHILD. HIS MIND IS CLOSED.

WE'LL FIND *ANOTHER* WAY TO REACH THE DAUPHIN.

I'VE FAILED!

MY *FIRST TASK*, AND I'VE FAILED!

1429.

I FAILED, FATHER. THESE PAST *FEW MONTHS* I'VE WRITTEN TO BAUDRICOURT, BUT HE HASN'T REPLIED TO MY LETTERS.

HE IS A MAN OF *ACTION*, MY CHILD. I FEAR WE MUST FIND A MORE *DIRECT* APPROACH.

PERHAPS IF YOU *ASK* FOR SOME ADVICE?

I WILL. BUT THE VOICES HAVE BEEN QUIET OF LATE.

BLESS ME, FATHER—

ARGH!!

YOU HAVE *DISPLEASED* US, CHILD. YOU HAVE *NOT SAVED FRANCE.* YOU HAVE STAYED AT HOME AND DONE *NOTHING.*

—HNF—
I AM A POOR GIRL. I DO NOT KNOW HOW TO RIDE OR FIGHT!

ALL YOU NEED TO DO IS SPEAK TO THE *DAUPHIN.*

HIS *SCOTTISH ALLIES* GROW BORED. THEY WILL CHARGE EARLY, AND THEY WILL *LOSE.*

YOU WILL PLAY YOUR PART. IT IS *GOD* WHO COMMANDS IT.

—SOB—

THY WILL BE DONE, LORD.

JEHANNE! WHAT HAVE YOU **DONE?** WHERE ARE YOU GOING?

BACK TO BAUDRICOURT, FATHER HUGO. I HAVE TO CHANGE HIS MIND. HE NEEDS TO **SEE THE TRUTH.**

MY TIME IS **RUNNING OUT.** THE VOICES TELL ME THAT THE DAUPHIN'S **SCOTTISH ALLIES** ARE ABOUT TO MAKE A **TERRIBLE MISTAKE** WHILE FIGHTING THE ENGLISH.

YOU CAN'T GO ALONE! AND WHERE'S YOUR **CLOAK?** IT'S JANUARY! YOU'LL CATCH YOUR DEATH IN THE COLD.

GOD'S LOVE WILL KEEP ME WARM, FATHER HUGO. AND AS FOR HAVING SOMEONE WITH ME...

...YOU'D BETTER RIDE **FASTER,** THEN!

COME ON! KEEP UP! YAAH!!

VAUCOULEURS.

DAMN THE SCOTS! THEIR PREMATURE ATTACK HAS MEANT THAT THE COUNT OF CLERMONT HAS HAD TO CEASE BOMBARDMENT.

CLERMONT IS A COWARD, SIR. ANY EXCUSE TO BACK AWAY FROM A FIGHT!

AND WHO SHOULD I SAY WISHES TO SPEAK TO HIM?

JEHANNE... NO. WAIT.

TELL HIM JOAN IS HERE.

A MESSENGER FROM DOMRÉMY, MY LORD. A "JOAN".

AS LONG AS IT ISN'T THAT MAD LITTLE GIRL AGAIN.

FIFTEEN LETTERS, THAT JEHANNE HAS SENT ME! I'VE HAD MORE LETTERS FROM HER THIS MONTH THAN FROM MY LOVERS!

THEN PERHAPS YOU SHOULD FIND SOME BETTER LOVERS, ROBERT.

YOU! WHAT THE HELL HAVE YOU DONE TO YOUR HAIR?

I SEE THE *SIEGE OF ORLÉANS* IS STILL GOING STRONG. LOOKS LIKE THERE ARE SOME *COMMUNICATION ISSUES* BETWEEN THE SCOTS AND THE COUNT OF CLERMONT.

I DON'T HAVE *TIME* FOR THIS! SOMEONE GET HER OUT OF HERE!

IF YOU *TOUCH* ME, THEN YOU WILL BE *DAMNED LIKE CAIN* – MARKED BY GOD AS A *TRAITOR* TO HIS CAUSE.

I AM HERE TO *HELP* YOU, ROBERT; TO SEE THE DAUPHIN BE CROWNED AT *REIMS*. AND TO PROVE MY WORTH...

...I WILL COMMUNE WITH *ANGELS*. I WILL GIVE YOU NEWS NOT YET KNOWN.

FINE, WHATEVER – TALK TO GOD AND THEN *GET OUT OF MY QUARTERS!*

I HAVE A MESSAGE FROM GOD. THE DAUPHIN'S FORCES HAVE THIS DAY SUFFERED A GREAT REVERSE NEAR ORLÉANS.

THE SCOTS HAVE BEEN HURT BADLY. THE ENGLISH HAVE *WON THE FIELD.*

I WILL WAIT OUTSIDE IN THE COURTYARD. YOUR ENVOYS WILL SOON CONFIRM MY WORDS.

WHEN THEY DO, PERHAPS *THEN* WE CAN DISCUSS WHETHER I AM *INSANE* OR NOT...

...AND WHAT *HELP* I CAN BE TO THE DAUPHIN, THE *TRUE* KING OF FRANCE.

MAKE WAY! I HAVE *IMPORTANT NEWS!*

CAPTAIN! THERE HAS BEEN A *TERRIBLE BATTLE!*

YOU. INSIDE. *NOW.*

THE COUNT OF CLERMONT WAS *TOO SLOW* TO HELP HIS SCOTTISH ALLIES, AND THEY WERE CUT DOWN BY THE ENGLISH.

THE SCOTTISH ATTACKED TOO SOON, THE *ARTILLERY* HAD TO STOP. THE ENGLISH WON.

FOUR HUNDRED MEN HAVE BEEN KILLED OR WOUNDED. *SIR JOHN STEWART*, THE LEADER OF THE SCOTS, IS DEAD. DUNOIS, THE *BASTARD OF ORLÉANS*, IS INJURED.

HOW DID YOU KNOW THIS?

I AM NOT YOUR *ENEMY*, ROBERT. I AM YOUR FRIEND, AND I BRING WITH ME *GREAT ALLIES.*

BUT MY WORDS ARE FOR THE *DAUPHIN ALONE.* CAN YOU HELP ME?

I AM A MILITARY MAN, JOAN. I BELIEVE IN WHAT I CAN.

AND CURRENTLY I SEE MY PEOPLE *DYING POINTLESSLY* IN A WAR THAT HAS GONE ON FOR TOO LONG.

IF YOU CAN PROMISE ME THAT YOU CAN ENSURE CHARLES IS CROWNED KING, THEN I WILL GIVE YOU A NOTE OF INTRODUCTION TO HIS COURT.

I CAN PROMISE YOU THIS, BECAUSE MY LIFE IS DEDICATED TO MAKING IT SO.

I GIVE YOU PASSAGE TO *CHINON*, WHERE YOU WILL FIND THE DAUPHIN. IT'S HOSTILE TERRITORY, SO STAY DRESSED LIKE A MAN.

I WILL PROVIDE YOU WITH AN ESCORT AND SEND ADVANCE NOTICE OF YOUR APPROACH.

THE DAUPHIN IS A *CAUTIOUS* MAN; I CANNOT GUARANTEE THAT HE WILL AGREE TO SEE YOU.

AN INTRODUCTION IS ALL I NEED, CAPTAIN.

GOD WILL PROVIDE THE REST.

HOW AMAZING THAT THE ANGELS CAN TELL YOU OF SUCH THINGS WELL BEFORE THEY HAPPEN!

TRULY A *MIRACLE!*

OH, MY *FATHER* HELPED ME - BUT *NOT* THE ONE YOU'RE THINKING OF, FATHER HUGO!

YEARS OF STANDING BESIDE MY FATHER AS HE PLANNED THE VILLAGE'S DEFENCES HAS GIVEN ME A *TACTICAL KNOWLEDGE* THAT I USED WHEN READING BAUDRICOURT'S MAP.

I SIMPLY *GUESSED* THE OUTCOME DRAWING ON MY OWN EXPERIENCE.

YOU *LIED!*

I HAD FAITH IN MY ANSWER, FATHER. ISN'T THAT ENOUGH?

THE VOICES DIDN'T HELP ME. LET'S HOPE THEY ARE MORE *ILLUMINATING* BY THE TIME WE REACH CHINON.

PERHAPS THEY DIDN'T GIVE YOU ALL THE FACTS BECAUSE THEY KNEW YOU'D FIND THE ANSWER ELSEWHERE?

QUITE POSSIBLLY. PERHAPS I CAN COMPLETE THIS TASK *WITHOUT* FOLLOWING MY PATH TO THE END.

PERHAPS THERE *IS A FUTURE* FOR ME...

THE LORD DOES MOVE IN *MYSTERIOUS WAYS,* MY CHILD!

YOU CAN'T BE *SERIOUS*, CHARLES! A *LUNATIC CHILD* SENT BY BAUDRICOURT IS NOT THE ANSWER. YOUR COMMANDERS WOULD LAUGH YOU OFF THE *FIELD OF BATTLE* IF THEY HEARD OF THIS!

SHE'S POSSESSED BY *DEVILS!* DEVILS THAT CONVINCED HIM TO GIVE HER PASSAGE.

ROBERT IS A FINE JUDGE OF CHARACTER, MOTHER. IF HE SAYS THAT WE SHOULD *SPEAK* TO THIS GIRL, THEN WE SHOULD. WHAT HAVE WE GOT TO LOSE?

IF SHE TRULY IS BLESSED BY GOD – OR EVEN IF SHE IS TOUCHED WITH SEEING THE FUTURE – IT WOULD BE OF *GREAT AID* TO FRANCE!

MY LORD, THE GIRL IS HERE.

EXCELLENT. KEEP HER WAITING. I HAVE A PLAN...

PIERRE, COME, SIT ON THE THRONE. BE *ME* FOR A MOMENT.

MY LORD? I DON'T UNDERSTAND.

WHEN THE GIRL ENTERS, SHE WILL APPROACH *YOU* – FOR *YOU* WILL BE ON THE THRONE.

BUT, IF GOD *REALLY* SPEAKS TO HER–

HE WILL LET HER KNOW OF THE *DECEPTION!* IF SHE FINDS THE TRUE CHARLES, SHE IS *LESS* OF A FRAUD.

LET'S SEE HOW GOOD HER "VOICES" ARE!

BEING LESS OF A FRAUD DOESN'T MEAN SHE *ISN'T* ONE, MOTHER.

SEND IN THE GIRL!

MY LORDS AND LADIES, *JOAN D'ARC*, AND *FATHER HUGO OF DOMRÉMY*.

MY LORD DAUPHIN, I THANK YOU SO MUCH FOR GRANTING US AN AUDIENCE! JOAN HERE IS SUCH A—

CEASE YOUR HONEYED WORDS, FATHER. *THAT'S* NOT THE DAUPHIN.

I ... WHAT ... ARE YOU *SURE*?

HOW DARE YOU SAY THAT! I SHOULD HAVE YOU ESCORTED OFF THE PREMISES!

YES, YOU *DO* THAT. IN THE MEANTIME, I'LL SEARCH OUT THE *TRUE* DAUPHIN...

...BECAUSE YOU'RE NOTHING BUT A *PALE IMITATION*.

MY LORD DAUPHIN. I ALMOST *MISSED* YOU IN THE CROWD.

INTERESTING ... SHE CERTAINLY FOUND YOU FAST ENOUGH! MAYBE SHE'S NOT AS MAD AS WE THOUGHT?

OR IT COULD HAVE BEEN THE *HALF A DOZEN PAINTINGS* OF ME SHE PASSED TO REACH THIS *VERY ROOM,* MOTHER!

I NEED MORE THAN THAT, I'M AFRAID!

IF YOU GIVE ME LEAVE TO SPEAK TO YOU *PRIVATELY,* MY LORD...

...I CAN OFFER YOU MORE. SOMETHING *ONLY YOU* KNOW.

EVERYONE AWAY! I WANT TO SEE THIS MAGIC TRICK.

COME ON! EVEN YOU, MOTHER.

YOU WORRY ABOUT YOUR *LEGITIMACY.* WHETHER YOU TRULY ARE YOUR *FATHER'S SON.*

MY FATHER TELLS YOU TO WORRY NO MORE. *YOU ARE HE.*

HOW DID— *NOBODY* KNOWS THAT I HAVE WORRIED ABOUT THIS!

I DO NOT SEEK *GLORY*; I DO NOT DESIRE *RICHES*. I AM MORE THAN JUST A MESSENGER FROM GOD, I AM A *FIGHTER*, A *PATRIOT FOR FRANCE* AND I HAVE TWO TASKS.

FIRSTLY, TO LIFT THE SIEGE AT ORLÉANS, HELD THESE LAST FIVE MONTHS.

SECONDLY, TO LEAD THE DAUPHIN TO REIMS FOR HIS *CORONATION AND ANOINTING*.

GOD KNOWS, MY LIEGE.

REIMS? THAT'S UNDER *ENGLISH CONTROL*. IT'LL NEVER HAPPEN.

I'M THE *ARCHBISHOP* THERE AND I'VE NOT SET FOOT IN MY CATHEDRAL FOR *YEARS*.

THEN I WILL HAVE TO WORK *HARDER* TO MAKE IT SO, WON'T I?

AND YOU WILL HELP, *RENAULT DE CHARTRES*, FOR GOD HAS *TOLD* ME ABOUT YOU. AFTER ALL, YOU WILL BE THE ONE WHO CROWNS THE KING!

I NEED TO DECIDE WHETHER THIS GIRL IS A *PROPHET* OR A *MADWOMAN POSSESSED BY DEVILS*.

CHANCELLOR, TAKE HER TO THE *NUNS AT POITIERS. EXAMINE* HER. TEST HER. MAKE YOUR DECISIONS. IF SHE SPEAKS FOR GOD, THEN WE CAN USE HER TO INSPIRE OUR SOLDIERS.

IF SHE FAILS, THEN SHE IS A *WITCH. A HERETIC*. AND SHE WILL *BURN*.

JOAN, YOU'VE IMPRESSED US ALL. WE TRULY BELIEVE THAT YOU HAVE THE *VOICE OF GOD* TO GUIDE YOU.

WITH YOUR HELP, WE CAN FINALLY REGAIN *ORLÉANS* – AND I CAN BE CROWNED *KING.*

I THEREFORE MAKE YOU, *JOAN D'ARC,* ONE OF MY KNIGHTS. AND WITH SUCH STANDING COMES A SWORD—

FORGIVE ME, SIRE, BUT THIS IS *NOT* THE SWORD I MUST TAKE.

I AM HERE TO LEAD, TO BE AN *EXAMPLE,* AND MY SWORD MUST BE A SYMBOL OF *EQUAL WORTH.*

I KNOW WHERE ONE SUCH SWORD LIES – BEHIND THE ALTAR IN THE *CHURCH OF SAINT CATHERINE OF FIERBOIS.*

IMPOSSIBLE! HOW CAN YOU BE CERTAIN THAT SUCH A SWORD EXISTS?

AND THAT IT WILL STILL BE THERE AFTER *SO MANY CENTURIES?*

OH, MY LORD, HAVEN'T YOU GUESSED?

SAINT CATHERINE HERSELF TOLD ME.

THE CHURCH OF SAINT CATHERINE OF FIERBOIS.

THE VOICES TOLD ME THE SWORD WOULD BE BEHIND THE ALTAR.

I KNOW YOU'RE THE *DUKE OF ALENÇON,* BUT COULD YOU *HELP* HERE?

OF COURSE, MY DEAR. AND PLEASE, CALL ME *JEAN.*

IT'S RUDE TO INSIST ON TITLES WITH A GIRL WHO SPEAKS WITH *GOD,* NO?

PUT YOUR BACKS INTO IT - HNF -!

THIS WEIGHS A TON! I HOPE YOU'RE CORRECT.

THERE'S NOTHING HERE! YOUR VOICES WERE *WRONG!*

DID YOU THINK IT WOULD SIMPLY BE *RESTING* THERE FOR ME?

SACRED OBJECTS SUCH AS THIS MUST BE FOUND. *EARNED.*

SHE NEEDS A BANNER PEOPLE CAN FOLLOW.

HOW ABOUT A PAINTING OF *GOD IN HEAVEN*, FLANKED BY ANGELS!

AND ADD THE WORDS *"JHESUS MARIA"*!

THAT'S IT, *JOAN!* HOLD THE REINS!

IN A BATTLE YOU *CAN'T* ALLOW THEM TO DISLODGE YOU FROM YOUR STEED. GOD CAN'T STOP YOU FALLING OFF A HORSE!

YOUR MEN ARE READY TO RIDE TO *ORLÉANS*, MA'AM.

JUST GIVE THE WORD AND WE'LL LEAVE.

MY DEAR DUKE.

MOUNT UP.

ORLÉANS.

WE'VE DESTROYED THE BRIDGE TO *LES TOURELLES*, IF WE CAN JUST WAIT IT OUT A LITTLE LONGER...

MORE THAN *SIX MONTHS* YOU'VE BEEN SAYING THIS, DUNOIS! THE PEOPLE OF ORLÉANS ARE *STARVING!*

WE'RE CONSTANTLY ATTACKED BY THE ENGLISH, AND OUR FOOD SUPPLIES TAKEN FOR THEIR *OWN SOLDIERS.* EVEN ALL THE *RATS* HAVE BEEN EATEN BY NOW!

WE'RE *ALL* STARVING! DO YOU SEE ANY FOOD HERE? *NO!*

WE'RE TRYING TO MAKE A DEAL WITH THE *BURGUNDIANS*; PERHAPS IF THEY AGREE AND STEP BACK, THERE WILL BE *FEWER SOLDIERS* TO FIGHT THROUGH!

AND, OF COURSE, THE DAUPHIN SENDS US THE *MAID*, THE MESSENGER FROM GOD, RATHER THAN SUPPLIES.

PRAISE BE TO HEAVEN. WE ARE SAVED!

WHAT DO YOU MEAN – *MAID*?

SPEAK CLEARER, GILLES!

HAVE YOU NOT HEARD? CHARLES SENDS *JOAN D'ARC*, A *PROPHET* WITH AN ARMY OF CLERGYMEN AND *ROYAL GUARD!*

SHE'S SUPPOSED TO END THE SIEGE. I JUST HOPE SHE BRINGS SOME *BREAD!*

TAKE COVER! THE ENGLISH ARE FIRING THE CATAPULTS *AGAIN!*

SHE SPEAKS TO *GOD*, THEY SAY. AND SHE WANTS THE ENGLISH GONE.

SHE'S ALREADY WRITTEN TWO LETTERS TO THE ENGLISH COMMANDER, *TALBOT*, TELLING HIM TO SURRENDER AND LEAVE!

WRITING LETTERS? *TRULY* THE WORK OF A *WOMAN*. STILL, IF SHE BRINGS US *ANY* SOLDIERS AND SUPPLIES, SHE'LL BE WELL RECEIVED.

A GIRL AS PERSISTENT AS THIS JOAN SOUNDS COULD BE *GOOD* FOR MORALE. ALREADY, THE TROOPS *TALK* ABOUT HER.

LET'S HOPE SHE ARRIVES *SOON* – WE MAY NEED HER PRAYERS QUICKER THAN SHE THINKS.

DAMN THIS WEATHER! MY ARMOUR WILL RUST.

WHERE *IS* THIS GIRL? I'M NOT WAITING HERE ALL DAY!

PATIENCE, MY FRIEND! LOOK, THE SKY CLEARS; THE SUN SHINES...

...OUR *SAVIOUR* ARRIVES!

THAT *HAD* TO BE STAGED.

TELL ME SHE WAITED UNTIL THE SUN CAME OUT!

JEAN! GILLES! THEY LEFT *YOU* IN CHARGE OF ORLÉANS? NO WONDER YOU NEEDED OUR HELP!

IS THAT THE *DUKE OF ALENÇON*? I HEARD YOU WERE DEAD!

NO, WAIT – *HOPED.* HOPED YOU WERE DEAD!

YOU JUST LACK *FAITH,* GILLES!

MAY I INTRODUCE JOAN D'ARC, THE MESSENGER FROM GOD!

JOAN, THESE REPROBATES ARE *JEAN, THE BASTARD OF ORLÉANS*; AND CAPTAIN *GILLES DE RAIS.*

MY LORD, WHERE IS *TALBOT*? I SENT HERALDS AHEAD STATING THAT I WISHED TO SPEAK TO HIM.

WELL, WE'VE DESTROYED THE BRIDGE THAT WOULD HAVE TAKEN HIM, AND THERE'S NO WIND TO SAIL THE BARGES ACROSS.

SO I'M AFRAID *THAT'S* OUT OF THE QUESTION.

HOW *DARE* YOU COUNTERMAND MY ORDERS! WHY DID WE MEET ON *THIS* SIDE OF THE LOIRE?

WE COULD HAVE MET ON THE *OTHER* SIDE AND GONE TOGETHER TO SEE HIM!

AYE, AND BEEN *KILLED* TOGETHER! YOU MIGHT BE A MESSENGER FROM GOD, GIRL...

...BUT TO THE ENGLISH YOU'RE JUST A *WITCH WITH A BANNER!*

AT LEAST COME TO ORLÉANS AND REST BEFORE WE WORK OUT WHAT TO DO NEXT!

WHAT TO DO NEXT? WHY IS THAT DIFFICULT? WE *ATTACK!*

WE ATTACK LES TOURELLES *IMMEDIATELY!*

I WISH JOAN LUCK. SHE'S A FIREBRAND. AND SHE'LL GET HER OWN WAY.

I HAVE NO DOUBT.

SO, HOW LONG *DID* YOU WAIT BEHIND THE RIDGE UNTIL THE SUN SHONE?

I HAVE NO IDEA WHAT YOU MEAN, BROTHER.

...

ABOUT *TWO HOURS!*

HA HA HA!

LATER. ORLÉANS.

EXCELLENT. NOW LET ME *SIGN* IT AND THEN PASS THIS TO THE WATCH COMMANDER.

I WANT THIS MESSAGE FIRED ACROSS TO THE ENGLISH.

YES, MA'AM.

MESSAGE FOR LORD TALBOT!

RECEIVED!

THAT'S WHAT WE THINK OF YOUR OFFER TO LET US SURRENDER!

WHEN WE CAPTURE YOUR WITCH, WE'LL BURN HER!

THEY'RE FIRING FLAMING ARROWS AT US IN RESPONSE TO A MESSAGE YOU SENT!

WHAT DID YOU SAY?

I SIMPLY GAVE TALBOT ONE LAST CHANCE TO *LEAVE*! WHY ARE YOU SO ANGRY?

BECAUSE YOU'VE *STIRRED THEM UP*, YOU FOOL!

THEY *WANT* A FIGHT, AND NOW WE'LL HAVE TO GIVE IT TO THEM.

GOOD! WE *NEED* TO ATTACK. WE START TOMORROW.

LOVED BY GOD OR NOT, I SWEAR I WILL PUT AN ARROW IN HER MYSELF!

WE SET OFF TOMORROW MORNING, BUT *NOT* WITH HER.

DON'T BE *HEROES*. WE'RE JUST GIVING THE ENGLISH A BLOODY NOSE.

UNDERSTAND?

WHAT OF JOAN?

OH, HER RIDE TOOK TOO MUCH OUT OF HER. I THOUGHT IT PRUDENT TO LET HER *SLEEP IN* TODAY.

SHE WON'T BE *HAPPY* WITH YOU.

THEN SHE CAN JOIN THE LIST. I'M NOT HERE TO BE *LIKED*, GILLES...

...I'M HERE TO KEEP MY PEOPLE *ALIVE*.

THE WALLS OF LES TOURELLES.

FOR FRANCE!

HURRY! I CAN FEEL DEATH IN THE AIR!

TAKE THE BUNDLES OF STICKS! *FILL THE MOAT WITH WOOD!*

MAKE *BRIDGES* TO CROSS ON!

MY LADY! DON'T FORGET YOUR *BANNER!*

I'M SORRY FOR NOT WAKING YOU. THE BASTARD OF ORLÉANS ORDERED US NOT TO.

HE *DID*, DID HE?

THEN THE FOOL WILL LOSE THE BATTLE.

I HAVE TO GET THERE BEFORE HE *RUINS* EVERYTHING!

THE WALLS OF LES TOURELLES.

IT'S *NO USE!* THERE ARE *TOO MANY* OF THEM. OUR LINES ARE BREAKING! OUR SOLDIERS ARE FLEEING.

WE SHOULD HAVE BROUGHT THE GIRL AND HER CLERICS – THEY COULD AT LEAST HAVE GIVEN US *LAST RITES!*

WE WERE *SO CLOSE.*

SOUND THE RETREAT!

LOOK! WE'RE SAVED!

MY LORD, I FEAR IT IS A **MORTAL** WOUND! I'VE SEEN MEN DIE FROM FAR LESS.

THE BEST I CAN DO IS MAKE HER **COMFORTABLE** - SHE WON'T LAST THE DAY!

I CAN'T ... HEAR ... WHAT DID ... HE SAY...?

YOU NEED TO REST, JOAN. HERE, TAKE THIS...

...IT'S AN **OPIATE** - A DRUG THAT WILL **NUMB** ALL PAIN.

NO ... NEED CLEAR HEAD ... FOR FIGHTING...

THERE'S NO MORE FIGHTING FOR **YOU**, DEAR GIRL.

JUST **GLORY** AT THE LORD'S SIDE.

STOP ... STANDING AROUND ... GO ... FIGHT...

...

SHE'S GONE.

THE MAID OF ORLÉANS IS DEAD.

AM I DEAD? IS THIS *HEAVEN*?

YES, YOU ARE DEAD, JOAN...

...BUT NO, THIS IS *NOT* HEAVEN.

YOUR MISSION IS NOT YET ACCOMPLISHED, MY CHILD. BUT YOU HAVE PASSED ON.

SOMEONE ELSE WILL CONTINUE WHAT YOU HAVE BEGUN. YOU CAN REST.

PLEASE! DON'T STOP ME NOW! WE'RE *SO CLOSE!*

SEND ME BACK. I CAN *DO THIS!* I'LL ACCEPT WHATEVER PENANCE IT TAKES.

IF YOU RETURN, YOUR END IS WRITTEN. *FIRE AND PAIN — YOU WILL BE BURNT AS A WITCH.*

ARE YOU *SURE* YOU WANT THAT?

DO I WANT THAT? NO. I'VE NEVER WANTED SOMETHING *LESS* IN ALL MY LIFE.

BUT IF I DON'T RETURN, THEN *FRANCE WILL FALL.* AND SAVING THIS REALM IS MORE IMPORTANT THAN ONE PEASANT GIRL.

SEND ME BACK, LORD...

...I BEG YOU, SEND ME BACK!

SHE'S *AWAKE!* MEN! SHE'S CONSCIOUS!

YOU *DIED,* JOAN.

WELL, WE *THOUGHT* YOU HAD. THE PHYSICIAN SAID HE COULD STILL HEAR A *HEARTBEAT,* SO HE PATCHED YOU UP AND LET YOU SLEEP.

AND THE BATTLE? DOES IT STILL GO ON?

NO. THE ENGLISH BEAT US; WE RETREATED AFTER YOUR INJURY. THE SOLDIERS FELT IT WAS A *BAD OMEN.*

PERFECT. HELP ME – HNG – UP!

FETCH MY ARMOUR!

IT'S LATE AT NIGHT; THE MEN ARE RESTING.

ARE YOU *INSANE?* WE CAN'T DO ANYTHING UNTIL DAWN. IT'S TOO DARK!

THEN WE MAKE IT *BRIGHTER.*

IT IS A *FULL MOON,* YES? THEN GOD WILL CLEAR THE CLOUDS, AND IT WILL BE AS BRIGHT AS DAY TO US.

IF WE ATTACK *NOW,* THE ENGLISH WILL BE DRUNK. SLEEPING.

UNPREPARED.

CHINON.

MY LORD DAUPHIN, I BRING NEWS FROM ORLÉANS.

JOAN HAS **BROKEN THE SIEGE!** THE ENGLISH HAVE SURRENDERED THE CITY!

I **KNEW** THAT SENDING HER WOULD BE A BLESSING! WITH HER TO INSPIRE THE TROOPS, AND WITH MEN LIKE THE BASTARD, GILLES, JEAN...

WE COULD WIN BACK ALL OF FRANCE!

PARIS SHOULD BE NEXT - IT'S CLOSE TO ORLÉANS, THEY CAN **REST** BEFORE THEY MOVE ON—

OH NO, MA'AM! THEY'VE ALREADY MOVED ON!

THEY MARCH TO **JARGEAU!** JOAN AIMS TO CLEAR THE **LOIRE VALLEY** OF ALL ENGLISH GARRISONS.

AND WHEN THAT TASK IS COMPLETE, THEY HEAD FOR **REIMS!**

REIMS? THAT'S **TWICE** AS FAR AS PARIS!

AND AS THEY MARCH, THE ENGLISH WILL HAVE TIME TO SUMMON REINFORCEMENTS!

SHE'S DOING WHAT SHE SWORE SHE WOULD, MOTHER. SHE'S ENSURING THAT I WILL BE CROWNED AT REIMS.

THE **MAID OF ORLÉANS** IS MORE THAN JUST A SIMPLE PEASANT GIRL NOW - SHE IS A **MIRACLE** WORKER.

LET US LEAVE HER TO CREATE **MORE** MIRACLES FOR FRANCE.

WITH THE BRIDGE AT ORLÉANS *DESTROYED*, AND THE OTHER CROSSINGS LOST, THIS IS THE *ONLY ROUTE* NORTH OF THE RIVER.

THERE ARE THREE MAIN AREAS: THE *BRIDGE FORTIFICATION*, THE *CITY* AND THE *CASTLE* ON THE EDGE.

WE DON'T HAVE THE MANPOWER TO CONDUCT A SIEGE, JOAN. AND THE CASTLE WILL BE A NIGHTMARE TO BREAK DOWN.

IT WOULD STOP THE ENGLISH FROM REACHING THE *SOUTH OF FRANCE*, THOUGH.

TRUE. BUT AT WHAT COST?

THE PROBLEM WITH YOU, GENTLEMEN, IS THAT YOU THINK LIKE *KNIGHTS*. LIKE *LORDS*.

I GREW UP LEARNING STRATEGY FROM A *VILLAGE MILITIA*. WE ALWAYS LOOKED AT THE *SMALLER* PICTURE.

THE CITY *SURVIVES* BY FORAGING SOUTH OF THE RIVER, RIGHT?

THEN WE SIMPLY TAKE THE BRIDGE. INSTALL A GARRISON. *STOP* THE ENGLISH.

NO FOOD – NO FIGHT.

MY GOD, IT'S SO *SIMPLE!* WE COULD DO IT TONIGHT!

THEN *DO* IT TONIGHT. AND SET UP CANNON TO BLAST ACROSS THE LOIRE AT THE CASTLE.

WE CAN'T LET THE ENGLISH SOLDIERS FEEL *FORGOTTEN* NOW, CAN WE?

LOCHES.

AND THEN THEY SIMPLY ESTABLISHED A GARRISON ON THE *SOUTH SIDE!*

THE ENGLISH WOKE UP TO FIND THEY HAD NO WAY SOUTH – THE CITY NEEDED SUPPLIES FROM THE FIELDS!

WHILE THE SOLDIERS HID IN THE CASTLE, *THE CITY MADE A DEAL WITH JOAN!*

AND WHAT *FOOLISHNESS* IS THIS?

WHERE DO YOU GO NOW?

TO *LOIRE*, MOTHER! TO JOAN!

SHE LEADS FRANCE TO VICTORY...

...AND I'LL BE DAMNED IF I'M *NOT THERE WHEN IT HAPPENS!*

DON'T SHOOT IT! LET IT RUN FREE.

THIS IS A MESSAGE FROM GOD!

IT'S A MESSAGE THAT REMINDS ME I HAVEN'T *EATEN* TODAY!

STAG! HO!

WILL YOU BE QUIET, YOU FOOLS! YOU'LL BE HEARD FOR MILES!

STAG!

DID I HEAR RIGHT? *ENGLISH VOICES* JUST OVER THAT RISE?

DISTRACTED ENGLISH VOICES WHO DON'T KNOW WE'RE HERE!

8 SEPTEMBER. THE ASSAULT ON PARIS.

I TELL YOU, JEAN, NOW HE'S KING, CHARLES DOESN'T SEEM *INTERESTED* IN WAR!

HIS DIPLOMATS FAILED, SO WHERE ARE THE *TROOPS* HE PROMISED US?

WHY DO *YOU* CARE, JOAN? YOUR JOB IS DONE. YOU HAD TWO TASKS TO FULFIL...

...FREE ORLÉANS AND CROWN CHARLES! *GO HOME! HAVE A FAMILY.*

AND YET STILL I HEAR THE *LORD'S VOICE* TELLING ME TO CONTINUE—

MY SWORD! I FORGOT TO BRING SAINT CATHERINE'S SWORD!

HERE, TAKE *THIS* ONE. HE DOESN'T HAVE NEED OF IT ANY MORE!

LOOK OUT - *ARGH!*

13 SEPTEMBER. THE ABBEY OF SAINT-DENIS.

JOAN? THE CONVOY IS LEAVING. WE NEED TO GET MOVING.

I KNOW, I JUST NEEDED TO BE *ALONE* FOR A MOMENT.

I THOUGHT OF ALL OF US, YOU WERE THE ONE WHO WAS *NEVER* ALONE.

IS THIS THE *SWORD* I FOUND FOR YOU? YOU'RE LEAVING IT HERE?

IT'S CUSTOMARY TO LEAVE AN OFFERING. I FELT IT WAS A WORTHY ONE.

AFTER ALL, THE *KING* DOESN'T THINK ME WORTHY ENOUGH TO WIELD IT.

GO BACK TO YOUR WIFE, JEAN. BE WITH HER THIS WINTER. FOR, IN SPRING, THIS TRUCE WILL FALL...

...AND I WILL BE AT WAR AGAIN. MY *TRUE SWORD* WILL BE UNSHEATHED ONCE MORE.

HOW DO YOU *KNOW* THIS? THE VOICES? GOD HIMSELF?

WHAT HAS HE SAID?

THE SAME AS HE *ALWAYS* DOES. THAT I WILL BE CAPTURED BY THE ENGLISH BEFORE *MIDSUMMER*...

...AND DEAD WITHIN TWO YEARS.

AUTUMN. BOURGES.

MY LORD, WHY HAVE YOU **FORSAKEN** ME?

WHY WON'T YOU SPEAK?

LOIRE.

THIS TREATY IS GOOD FOR **BOTH** SIDES. FOR IF FRANCE AND BURGUNDY CONTINUE THIS ALLIANCE...

...THEN THE ENGLISH CAN **NEVER** WIN.

WINTER.

SO THE KING MADE YOU A **NOBLEWOMAN**? THAT IS A FINE REWARD.

DO YOU STILL HEAR THE VOICES?

NO, FATHER, NOT FOR MANY MONTHS NOW.

I KNOW THAT THIS TREATY IS **WRONG**. THE BURGUNDIANS WILL ALLY THEMSELVES AGAIN WITH THE ENGLISH.

BUT THE KING WILL NOT **LISTEN** TO ME. HE GIVES ME **TITLES** INSTEAD OF **SOLDIERS**.

HE SAYS DIPLOMACY IS **CHEAPER** THAN WAR.

BUT HE STILL BLAMES ME FOR **PARIS**. HE STILL BLAMES ME FOR FAILING.

AND **SO** DOES GOD.

SPRING. 1430.

BLESS ME, FATHER, FOR I HAVE—

WHY ARE YOU **HERE**, JOAN? **WHY DO YOU NOT FIGHT?**

HOW YOU DIE IS SET IN STONE. HOW YOU *LIVE* UNTIL THEN ISN'T.

WITH WHAT? THE KING GIVES ME *NOTHING*. AND YOU CLAIM THAT I WILL BE DEAD IN JUST OVER A YEAR – BURNT AS A *WITCH*!

CHARLES BELIEVES IN DIPLOMACY, BUT THE TRUCE HAS EXPIRED AND THE BURGUNDIANS *BETRAY* HIM! THEY SIDE WITH BEDFORD AND THE ENGLISH. THEY MARCH FOR *COMPIÈGNE*!

YOU WILL *FIGHT*, JOAN. AND YOU WILL BE *CAPTURED*...

...BUT YOUR SELFLESS ACT WILL CHANGE FRANCE FOR EVER!

22 MAY 1430. CHINON.

WHAT NEWS?

THE BURGUNDIANS HAVE *BROKEN THE TREATY*, YOUR MAJESTY! PHILIP THE GOOD OF BURGUNDY HAS SIDED WITH BEDFORD OF ENGLAND.

THEY *MARCH INTO FRANCE* AND AIM TO TAKE COMPIÈGNE! *COUNT JEAN OF LIGNY* JOINS THEM WITH HIS MEN.

THAT CUR! WE'LL *NEVER* RAISE AN ARMY IN TIME TO BEAT THEM THERE!

I SHOULD HAVE LISTENED TO JOAN!

MY LIEGE ... JOAN IS ALREADY AT COMPIÈGNE!

SHE RAISED A FORCE OF *FOUR HUNDRED MEN* AND RODE THERE LAST WEEK.

FOUR HUNDRED AGAINST *SEVERAL THOUSAND*? SHE CAN'T DEFEAT THOSE ODDS!

AND WE'LL *NEVER GET THERE IN TIME.*

FALL BACK TO THE CITY! WE CAN WAIT IT OUT UNTIL THE KING'S ARMY ARRIVES! GO!

COME ON, JOAN! HURRY!

NOT UNTIL MY MEN HAVE GONE THROUGH SAFELY!

ARCHERS, DEFEND THE MAID! DO NOT—

NO! WHY DID YOU LOWER THE PORTCULLIS?

I DIDN'T, CAPTAIN! THE ROPE JUST BROKE!

JOAN! THE PORTCULLIS IS JAMMED...!

STAY STRONG! WE'LL GET YOU A ROPE FROM THE BATTLEMENTS.

IT'S ALL RIGHT, CAPTAIN. THIS WAS SUPPOSED TO HAPPEN. IT'S GOD'S WILL.

MY LORD BEDFORD, I HAVE NEWS!

GO ON, THEN! OUT WITH IT, LAD!

THE WOMAN – JOAN THE MAID – SHE'S BEEN *CAPTURED!*

THEY TOOK HER AT COMPIÈGNE!

EXCELLENT! CALL THE PRIESTS. I WANT THEM TO DRAW UP *CHARGES OF HERESY!*

CONTACT HER GAOLERS. ASK THEM HOW MUCH THEY *WANT* FOR THE WITCH!

LORD BEDFORD! SHE'S A *CHILD!*

SHE'S NOT A CHILD, WALLACE. SHE'S A *MILITARY* COMMANDER. SO TREAT HER LIKE ONE.

CHARLES STAGED HIS *CORONATION* ON THE BACK OF HER VISIONS. IF SHE IS DISCREDITED, THEN *SO IS HE.*

BUT STILL, THE KING SHOULD BE MADE AWARE—

THE KING IS CURRENTLY AN *EIGHT-YEAR-OLD BOY* WHO DOESN'T EVEN KNOW *WHY HE IS IN FRANCE!*

WE WILL BUY THE MAID OF ORLÉANS, AND WE WILL TRY HER. DISCREDIT HER.

AND THEN WE WILL *BURN* HER.

OCTOBER 1430. THE FORTRESS OF BEAUREVOIR.

FOOD FOR YOU ... LADY JEANNE SAID WE HAD TO TREAT YOU PROPERLY.

SO HOW ABOUT YOU *RETURN THE FAVOUR* AND TAKE OFF THAT STUPID UNIFORM? WE HAVE PLENTY OF LOVELY *DRESSES* YOU COULD WEAR!

THANK YOU, BUT I CANNOT. GOD HASN'T GIVEN ME *LEAVE* TO CHANGE MY CLOTHES.

YOUR DECISION. BUT IT MIGHT BE *TAKEN* FROM YOU SOON. I HEARD BURGUNDY'S NEGOTIATING WITH THE *ENGLISH.*

THEY'RE OFFERING A *LOT OF MONEY* FOR YOU.

BUT THAT ISN'T HOW RANSOMS WORK! FRANCE PAYS THE RANSOM! I DON'T GET SOLD TO A *BETTER BUYER!*

THE ENGLISH DON'T WANT YOU TAKING THE FIELD AGAIN.

AND THEIR POCKET IS *BIGGER* THAN YOUR KING'S.

I WILL NOT BE SOLD TO THE ENGLISH!

I'D RATHER DIE THAN BE SOLD TO THE ENGLISH!

I'D RATHER DIE.

APPARENTLY JOAN WAS INJURED WHILE TRYING TO *ESCAPE*. ALTHOUGH FALLING SIXTY FEET OFF A BALCONY SOUNDS MORE LIKE A *SUICIDE ATTEMPT*.

BECAUSE OF THIS, LIGNY HAS *ACCEPTED* THE ENGLISH OFFER OF *TEN THOUSAND GOLD CROWNS* FOR HER.

WE *CAN'T* LET THAT HAPPEN, YOUR MAJESTY!

DO YOU THINK I *WANT* IT TO? WE *DON'T HAVE* TEN THOUSAND GOLD CROWNS! WE'RE BARELY HOLDING ON HERE!

WE CAN'T RAISE AN ARMY OVER ONE GIRL – EVEN *THIS* GIRL! MY CROWN TEETERS ON A *KNIFE EDGE* AT THE MOMENT!

THEN WHY *CALL ME HERE*, SIRE?

BECAUSE THERE ARE *OTHER* WAYS TO FIGHT THIS. THE ENGLISH WANT TO TRY JOAN FOR *HERESY*.

IF JOAN IS BRANDED A *WITCH*, AND I TOOK *ADVICE* FROM HER? I'D LOSE THE BACKING OF THE CHURCH.

IT WOULD WEAKEN MY HOLD ON FRANCE, AND MAKE THE CLAIM OF ENGLAND'S HENRY STRONGER.

AND THE ENGLISH WOULD *OWN* HIM.

THEY WISH TO HOLD THE TRIAL IN *ROUEN*, BUT HAVE AGREED TO HAVE AS MANY FRENCH CLERGY AS ENGLISH THERE.

OFFICIALLY THEY'LL BE THERE FOR THE SAME REASON – THE CHARGE OF *HERESY*. BUT UNOFFICIALLY? THEY'LL BE TRYING TO FIND A *LOOPHOLE* TO FREE JOAN.

I WANT YOU TO ACCOMPANY THE *DOMINICAN YSAMBARD DE LA PIERRE* THERE. I WANT YOU TO BE A COMFORT TO JOAN. TELL HER...

...TELL HER I WISH I COULD HAVE *DONE MORE*.

TELL HER IT'S IN *GOD'S* HANDS NOW.

24 FEBRUARY 1431. ROUEN.

DO YOU KNOW WHETHER OR NOT YOU ARE IN *GOD'S GRACE*?

IF I AM NOT, MAY GOD PUT ME THERE. AND IF I AM, MAY GOD SO *KEEP* ME THERE.

I SHOULD BE THE *SADDEST CREATURE IN THE WORLD* IF I KNEW I WERE NOT IN HIS GRACE.

ORDER! I SAY, ORDER!

A *GOOD ANSWER* – TO SAY YES WOULD MEAN SHE WAS PRESUMING TO KNOW THE MIND OF GOD.

TO SAY NO WOULD MEAN SHE WAS ADMITTING SHE HAD COMMITTED MORTAL SINS AND HAD NOT REPENTED THEM.

BOTH ANSWERS WOULD HAVE MADE HER GUILTY OF *HERESY*.

BOTH ANSWERS WOULD HAVE LED TO HER *DEATH*.

YOU DICTATED LETTERS: DURING *YOUR LOIRE* CAMPAIGN, AM I RIGHT?

ONE STATED *"BEFORE SEVEN YEARS* ARE PAST THE ENGLISH WILL LOSE A GREATER STAKE THAN THEY DID AT ORLÉANS, FOR THEY WILL LOSE *EVERYTHING IN FRANCE".*

HOW DO YOU KNOW THIS? AND WHAT DOES IT MEAN?

IT MEANS WHAT IT STATES. IN LESS THAN SEVEN YEARS *PARIS* WILL FALL. THE ENGLISH WILL LOSE *EVERYTHING* IN FRANCE.

HOW DO I KNOW? *GOD* HAS TOLD ME.

YOUR APPARITIONS ... WERE THEY MALE? FEMALE? DID THEY HAVE HAIR?

SAINT MARGARET – DIDN'T SHE SPEAK ENGLISH?

WHY SHOULD SHE SPEAK ENGLISH WHEN SHE ISN'T ON THE *ENGLISH* SIDE?

YOU MENTION A *SIGN* THAT YOU GAVE TO THE KING, SO THAT HE WOULD KNOW THE TRUTH OF YOUR WORDS.

WHAT WAS THAT SIGN?

GO AND ASK *HIM.*

THE COMMON PEOPLE *LOVED* YOU, DID THEY NOT? THEY WOULD KISS YOUR HANDS, YOUR FEET, YOUR CLOTHES, YOUR RINGS...

...WHY DID THEY DO THIS? DID THEY THINK YOU COULD *HEAL THEM OF THEIR AILMENTS*?

MANY WOMEN TOUCHED MY HANDS AND MY RINGS, BUT I DO NOT KNOW WITH WHAT THOUGHT OR *INTENTION*, BISHOP CAUCHON.

AND I THINK IT'S SAFE TO SAY I NEVER CURED *ANYONE* WITH ANY OF MY RINGS.

COULD YOU CURE MY *BALDNESS* WITH YOUR RINGS?

THIS WHOLE TRIAL IS A *FARCE*. THE CHURCH TRIES TO SAVE ITS OWN...

...RATHER THAN DOING WHAT IT WAS *TOLD* AND HANDING HER OVER TO US.

YOU ALSO MET WITH *CATHERINE DE LA ROCHELLE*, A FRENCH MYSTIC WHO *ALSO* CLAIMS TO HAVE REVELATIONS FROM GOD.

SHE IS *NOTHING* – A FOLLY AND NOTHING MORE.

MY SAINTS TOLD ME SO.

WHILE YOU WERE AT *BEAUREVOIR* YOU LEAPED SIXTY FEET FROM A BALCONY. YOU WERE BADLY INJURED...

...BUT WERE YOU TRYING TO ESCAPE, OR *KILL* YOURSELF?

I LEAPED FROM FEAR OF THE ENGLISH, AND COMMENDED MYSELF TO GOD...

...FOR I WOULD RATHER *SURRENDER MY SOUL TO GOD* THAN FALL INTO THE HANDS OF THE ENGLISH.

I DON'T THINK THE GIRL *LIKES YOU*, MY LORD WARWICK.

SHE'LL LIKE ME EVEN *LESS* WHEN I *BURN HER.*

THIS FARCE IS *OVER* FOR THE DAY.

CAUCHON? I WOULD HAVE *WORDS* WITH YOU.

THE EARL OF WARWICK'S CHAMBERS.

WHOSE SIDE ARE YOU ON, CAUCHON?

WHY, THE CHURCH'S SIDE, MY LORD WARWICK.

WRONG. YOU'RE ON OUR SIDE, WHETHER YOU LIKE IT OR NOT.

ROUEN IS IN ENGLISH HANDS. WE ALLOW YOU TO PRESIDE OVER THIS TRIAL OUT OF THE GOODNESS OF OUR HEARTS.

IF YOU CARRY ON LIKE THIS, IT WON'T TAKE MUCH TO REMOVE YOU, AND FIND SOMEONE MORE SUITED TO THE TASK!

BUT, MY LORD ... THE HOLY ROMAN CHURCH...

THE POPE? IS HE HERE? UNDER THESE, PERHAPS? NO?

THE POPE BE DAMNED. HE'S NOT HERE. I AM. AND SO IS A GARRISON OF ENGLISH SOLDIERS WHO ALL WANT THAT WITCH DEAD.

DON'T DISAPPOINT US, BISHOP.

LET'S JUST SAY THAT YOUR SPIRITUAL FUTURE DEPENDS ON IT.

DAMN THAT INFERNAL ENGLISHMAN!

BISHOP? IS EVERYTHING ALL RIGHT?

YOU KNEW HER WHEN SHE WAS YOUNG, YES? WATCHED HER GROW UP?

HAS SHE *ALWAYS* BEEN THIS STUBBORN AND MULE-HEADED?

I'M AFRAID SO, YES. BUT SHE HAS ALSO ALWAYS BEEN *FAITHFUL* TO GOD AND THE CHURCH.

YOU ALMOST SOUND AS IF YOU *BELIEVE* HER, HUGO.

I SAW THINGS IN ORLÉANS THAT I CANNOT EXPLAIN, BISHOP. I NEVER SAW ANGELS, OR HEARD HER VOICES...

...BUT I TRULY BELIEVE THAT SOME *HIGHER POWER* WAS GUIDING HER AIM. AND GOD SEEMS THE BEST CHOICE.

HMM. WELL, WHATEVER THE TRUTH OF IT, TELL HER...

...TELL HER TO STOP MAKING A *MOCKERY* OF THE COURT – I *BEG* YOU!

23 MAY 1431.

SHE TWISTS OUR STATEMENTS AT EVERY TURN, AND ANSWERS A QUESTION WITH ANOTHER...

DO YOU HAVE A *VERDICT*? WHEN DO WE BURN HER?

IT'S NOT YET DECIDED IF SHE *IS* TO BE BURNED, MY LORD WARWICK. THE CHURCH HAS STRICT GUIDELINES—

TO HELL WITH YOUR GUIDELINES! I WANT HER BURNT TOMORROW!

MY LORD! IF YOU WANT HER TRIED BY THE CHURCH, THEN YOU HAVE TO *ABIDE BY OUR RULES!* UNLESS SHE *REFUSES TO RECANT* HER HERESY, SHE CANNOT BE BURNT.

IF YOU WANT ANOTHER VERDICT, THEN *TRY HER YOURSELF!*

MY MEN WILL NOT *FIGHT* UNTIL THEY KNOW THAT SHE IS *DEAD!*

FOR *MONTHS* YOU HAVE SAT AROUND THAT TABLE DOING *NOTHING*. WHY ARE YOU SCARED OF A *GIRL*?

IT'S NOT THE *GIRL* WE'RE SCARED OF; IT'S THE *VOICES*.

IF THEY'RE REAL, THEN WE ARE *ARGUING AGAINST GOD*. AND TO DO THAT IS TRULY THE WAY TO *DAMN YOUR SOUL*.

24 MAY.

FRANCE, THE BASTION OF TRUE CHRISTIANITY, MUST WEEP, FOR IT HAS BEEN ABUSED!

CHARLES, WHO CALLS HIMSELF *KING*, HAS FOLLOWED THE WORDS OF THIS *WORTHLESS WOMAN*, WHO IS FULL OF DISHONOUR!

I DENOUNCE YOU FOR HERESY!

BY MY FAITH, SIR, THERE IS NO *NOBLER CHRISTIAN TO BE FOUND* THAN THE KING.

SHAME ON YOU, FOR THE KING IS NOT LIKE YOU SAY. HE *LOVES* THE FAITH AND THE CHURCH.

WHY IS MY TRIAL NOT HEARD BY *ROME*? WHY DOES THE *POPE* NOT MAKE THE FINAL DECISION?

BECAUSE ROME IS *TOO FAR AWAY!* BAILIFF! PLEASE, SILENCE HER!

BUT ONE OF MY CHARGES WAS THAT I *REFUSED TO SUBMIT TO THE HOLY CHURCH OF ROME.*

IF I AM NOT *ABLE* TO FACE THEM, HOW CAN I *REFUSE?*

YOU ARE GUILTY OF **SO MANY SINS**. FIRST, THAT YOU **WORE AND STILL WEAR MEN'S CLOTHES**, AND YOUR HAIR **SHORT**, CLAIMING THAT GOD COMMANDED YOU SO.

YOU PRETENDED TO HAVE HAD **REVELATIONS AND APPARITIONS** OF GOD, THE ANGELS, SAINT CATHERINE AND SAINT MARGARET.

YOU BORE ARMS IN BATTLE, **CRUELLY DESIRING HUMAN BLOOD.**

YOU HAVE **DESPISED GOD AND HIS SACRAMENTS**, ADORED AND INVOKED **EVIL SPIRITS.**

THE LIST GOES ON. BUT THE CHURCH IS MERCIFUL. **RECANT YOUR SINS**, JOAN. APOLOGIZE.

REFUSE TO WEAR THESE CLOTHES AGAIN. **RENOUNCE HERESY** AND MAKE SUITABLE PENANCE...

...AND THE CHURCH WILL WELCOME YOU BACK INTO ITS BOSOM.

IF YOU SIGN THIS, THEY *CANNOT* BURN YOU. THE ENGLISH AND BURGUNDIANS *CANNOT KEEP* YOU.

YOU WILL BE *FREE*, JOAN, AS LONG AS YOU REPENT.

BUT WHAT OF MY VOICES?

ASK THEM. DO *THEY* TELL YOU NOT TO SIGN?

IF YOU DO NOT DO THIS, CHILD, THERE IS EVERY POSSIBILITY THAT THE ENGLISH WILL *BURN YOU RIGHT NOW.*

I DON'T KNOW HOW TO READ OR WRITE. IS THIS *MARK* ACCEPTABLE?

VERY.

YOU HAVE *RETURNED TO THE CHURCH*, CHILD. BUT YOU MUST PAY FOR YOUR CRIMES.

THE PENANCE IS *PERPETUAL IMPRISONMENT.*

WHAT? YOU SAID SHE WOULD *GO FREE!*

CAUCHON! YOU LIED! YOU BORE FALSE WITNESS!

YOU'LL BURN IN HELL!

DAMN *THIS DOCUMENT!* PERPETUAL IMPRISONMENT IS NOTHING – *I WANT HER DEAD!*

IF WE BURN HER NOW, SHE'S NOTHING BUT A *MARTYR*, AND CHARLES WILL GROW STRONGER!

SHE'S EVEN TAKEN TO WEARING A *DRESS!* SAYS THAT SHE'S *REPENTING!*

DON'T WORRY, MY LORD WARWICK, WE'LL GET HER YET.

LOOK...

...SEE HOW SHE *SIGNED* THIS? SHE CLAIMS SHE CANNOT READ OR WRITE.

YET SHE SIGNED HER NAME TO *EVERY LETTER* SHE SENT LORD TALBOT AT ORLÉANS!

SHE *PLAYS* WITH US! SHE'LL SOMEHOW FREE HERSELF AND THEN SHE'LL BE BACK IN ARMOUR FIGHTING US – NO MATTER WHAT THIS PIECE OF PAPER SAYS!

BUT WHAT IF SHE WAS TO BE FOUND IN MEN'S CLOTHES? TO BE SEEN *FLOUTING* THE *PENANCE* SHE SHOULD BE PERFORMING?

OH, TO GO AGAINST SUCH A DECREE AFTER WILLINGLY SIGNING IT, THAT WOULD BE *HERESY.*

MAKE IT SO.

30 MAY 1431. DAWN.

MY CHILD, HOW DID IT COME TO THIS?

HOW DID YOU *FALL* SO FAR?

THEY *TRICKED* ME – TORE MY CLOTHES OFF AND TOLD ME I WAS *DAMNED*.

WHAT DID YOU *THINK* I WOULD DO? I'M A *SOLDIER!*

NO, JOAN, YOU'RE JUST A GIRL.

A GIRL WITH AN *INCREDIBLE GIFT*, WHO HELPED FRANCE...

...BUT JUST A GIRL, STILL.

THEY'RE READYING THE PYRE AS WE SPEAK, JOAN. AT *TEN O'CLOCK* THIS MORNING THEY WILL TAKE YOU AND *EXECUTE* YOU.

AND THERE'S *NOTHING* I CAN DO TO STOP IT.

LET THEM BURN ME. I'VE KNOWN OF THIS FATE FOR *YEARS*. EVER SINCE ORLÉANS, AND THE ARROW.

IT'S NOT MY *PHYSICAL SELF* I'M WORRIED ABOUT, BISHOP CAUCHON...

...IT'S MY *SPIRITUAL SELF*.

I CAN'T GO TO THE PYRE WITHOUT *CONFESSION*, FATHER! I JUST CAN'T!

WOULD YOU *DAMN MY SOUL AND LEAVE ME TO THE ENGLISH?*

NO, MY CHILD. THE CHURCH WOULD *NEVER* DO THAT.

FATHER HUGO WILL HEAR YOUR FINAL CONFESSION.

THANK YOU, FATHER. I FEEL BETTER KNOWING THAT MY SOUL IS SAVED.

IT'LL BE A **COMFORT** WHEN I'M IN THE FLAMES.

JOAN, REMEMBER ORLÉANS? WHEN YOU HAD THE **ARROW** IN YOU?

I OFFERED YOU A **DRUG** — ONE THAT WOULD NUMB YOU FOR HOURS, **STOP ALL PAIN**. I COULD GIVE THAT TO YOU...

NO, FATHER, I COULD NEVER **WILLINGLY** TAKE SOMETHING LIKE THAT.

IT WOULD **LESSEN** MY SACRIFICE TO GOD.

I UNDERSTAND, MY CHILD.

THEN LET US HAVE ONE FINAL **DRINK** TOGETHER AS WE WAIT FOR THE SUN TO RISE. THE BISHOP PROVIDED SOME **WINE** FOR US.

I'VE KNOWN YOU ALL YOUR LIFE, CHILD. IT FEELS **WRONG** TO STAND HERE AT THE END.

THANK YOU, FATHER, FOR BEING THERE WITH ME. FOR ALWAYS BELIEVING IN ME.

OH, I'VE ALWAYS BEEN THERE, JOAN. FOLLOWING YOU, ADVISING YOU...

... **PROTECTING** YOU.

FORGIVE ME, LORD, BUT I **WILL NOT** LET HER SUFFER.

30 MAY. THE EXECUTION OF JOAN OF ARC.

DO YOU HAVE ANY FINAL WORDS OR REQUESTS?

YES. I CALL UPON THE **FATHER, SON AND THE HOLY SPIRIT.** I CALL UPON THE **BLESSED VIRGIN MARY** AND ALL THE SAINTS OF PARADISE.

PARDON MY JUDGES AND MY EXECUTIONER, FOR THEY **KNOW NOT** WHAT THEY DO.

I ASKED FOR A **CROSS** TO BE BROUGHT FROM SAINT SAUVEUR, SO I CAN SEE IT AS I END MY LIFE.

IS IT HERE?

YES, MY LADY. AND FOR WHAT IT'S WORTH...

...I'M SORRY.

DO YOUR DUTY.

LORD, LET THE *MEDICINE WORK*. LET HER BE *NUMB* FROM ALL PAIN.

IN THE NAME OF *JESUS!*

MICHAEL! YOU COME TO ME!

IT IS TIME TO *COME HOME*, CHILD. TO SIT AT THE SIDE OF THE LORD, *BASKING IN HIS GLORY.*

THIS TIME HAS BEEN WELL KNOWN AND *PREPARED FOR.* WHILE THE FLAMES TAKE THIS MOST *MORTAL* OF BODIES...

LATER.

HERE, FATHER — HER *ASHES*. THEY'RE TO BE SCATTERED OVER THE *SEINE*.

BUT THEY AGREED THAT *YOU* COULD DO IT IF YOU SO WISHED. AND WITH WHOMEVER YOU WANTED.

THANK YOU.

EVEN LATER.

THANK YOU FOR COMING; IT WOULD HAVE MEANT A LOT TO HER.

I CAN'T STAY LONG — BEING A *MARSHAL OF FRANCE* IS A VERY DEMANDING ROLE. BUT, FOR JOAN...

IT WAS THE *LEAST* I COULD DO. ORLÉANS OWES *EVERYTHING* TO HER.

ALL I HAVE TO GO BACK TO IS MORE FIGHTING IN NORMANDY.

I *ASKED* FOR HER, YOU KNOW. I WROTE TO CHARLES AND ASKED HIM TO SEND JOAN TO HELP ME.

IF I'D TRIED HARDER, SHE MIGHT HAVE *SURVIVED*.

DID NONE OF HER *FAMILY* WISH TO BE HERE?

NO, HER FATHER IS ILL IN DOMRÉMY. BESIDES, *YOU* WERE HER FAMILY WHEN IT MATTERED.

AND DON'T CHASTISE YOURSELF SO, JEAN. SHE *ALWAYS KNEW* THAT THIS WAS TO BE HER FATE.

"*IN THE SWEAT OF THY FACE SHALT THOU EAT BREAD, TILL THOU RETURN UNTO THE GROUND; FOR OUT OF IT WAST THOU TAKEN...*"

"*...AND UNTO DUST SHALT THOU RETURN.*"

GOODBYE, JEHANNE.

I SHOULD HAVE *LISTENED* TO YOU. IF I'D FOUND THE TROOPS, PERHAPS PARIS *WOULD* HAVE FALLEN.

PERHAPS THINGS WOULD HAVE BEEN *DIFFERENT*.

THE ENGLISH CROWNED HENRY *KING OF FRANCE* TODAY, JOAN.

THEY THINK *THIS* GIVES HIM LEGITIMACY OVER ME. THEY *IGNORE* MY CLAIM.

PERHAPS YOU'D STILL BE *ALIVE*.

I'M SO *SORRY*, JOAN...

YOU *NEVER* HAVE TO APOLOGIZE TO ME, MY KING.

WE ALL HAD OUR *PARTS TO PLAY*.

ARE YOU A GHOST? AN *ANGEL*?

NEITHER... JUST A *VISITOR*, SENT BY HER *LORD* TO CALM A MAN'S SPIRITS.

HELLO, CHARLES.

I ALWAYS KNEW MY *FATE*. FROM THE FIRST MOMENT THE VOICES SPOKE, I KNEW I WOULD *DIE YOUNG*. AND AT ORLÉANS I KNEW OF THE *FLAMES*.

IF I COULD RETURN AND DO IT AGAIN, I *WOULDN'T CHANGE A THING*.

BUT *YOU* NEED TO CHANGE. I GAVE YOU *FRANCE* AND THE ENGLISH *TAKE IT BACK*.

BE THE KING I *BELIEVED* IN, CHARLES. *TAKE PARIS*. REGAIN YOUR LANDS.

PARIS? IT'S *UNDEFEATABLE*! THE ENGLISH WILL NEVER LOSE IT!

I TOLD YOU ONCE THAT PARIS WOULD FALL WITHIN *SEVEN YEARS*. DO YOU *STILL NOT BELIEVE ME*?

I AM AT *PEACE* NOW, MY KING.

SO TOO MUST *YOU* BE – FOR *FRANCE*.

IN 1435 CHARLES MADE A *TREATY* WITH THE BURGUNDIANS, BREAKING ENGLAND'S HOLD ON FRANCE FOR EVER.

TWO YEARS LATER, HE *RECAPTURED* PARIS FROM THE ENGLISH – IN HONOUR OF JOAN.

IN 1449 HE REGAINED ROUEN AND THE FOLLOWING YEAR, WITH THE TRIAL RECORDS NOW HIS, DEMANDED A *RETRIAL* OF JOAN TO CLEAR HER NAME.

IN 1456 THE ORIGINAL VERDICT OF 1431 WAS *OVERTURNED* BY THE CHURCH, AND JOAN BECAME SEEN AS A MARTYR.

AFTER A *BEATIFICATION* IN 1909, JOAN OF ARC WAS MADE A *SAINT* IN 1920 BY *POPE BENEDICT XV.*

SAINT JOAN IS NOW A *PATRON SAINT OF FRANCE*, THE COUNTRY SHE *FOUGHT*, *SAVED* AND *DIED* FOR.

THE END.

TONY LEE

Tony Lee has written for many popular comic books including
X-Men, *Spider Man*, *Starship Troopers*, *Wallace & Gromit* **and** *Shrek*.
He is also the writer of the *Doctor Who* **comics series.**
His adaptation of *Pride & Prejudice & Zombies: The Graphic Novel*
is a *New York Times* **bestseller. Tony is the author of** *Outlaw:*
The Legend of Robin Hood **and** *Excalibur: The Legend of King Arthur*
both published by Walker Books. Tony lives in London.

SAM HART

Sam Hart is a comic book artist and magazine illustrator, having worked on *Starship Troopers* and *Judge Dredd* and for publishers Markosia and DC Comics, amongst others. He is the illustrator of *Outlaw: The Legend of Robin Hood* and *Excalibur: The Legend of King Arthur* which are published by Walker Books. Born in England, Sam now lives and teaches comic art in Brazil.

STRONG BACK
OPEN FRONT

John Howe . 2011
AFTER
GERALDINE FARRAR

Acknowledgements

With my loving thanks to many friends, among them:
Sasha Hart, Juliana Taioli and Lucas Taioli Hart,
Tamara Katzenstein, Suzana Katzenstein, Miriam Markus,
Daniel Markus, Elia Fernaldes, Frances Hollis, Flavio Luiz,
Eduardo and Manoela Schaal, Susana Salomão, Eduardo Gomes,
Sylvio Mello, Antonio Americo, Marcelo Campos, Igor Pessoa,
Mauricio Mudrik, Bia Cortese and Luiza Mudrik, Carlos Livieres,
Carol Lefevre, Sheila Finger, Octavio Cariello, Gualberto Costa
and Daniela Baptista, Rodrigo Reis, Soraya Lucato, Mario Colombo,
Jan Rocha and Lise Forell.
                                                    S. H.